Solve-It-Yourself
Mysteries

Hy Conrad & Bob Peterson

Illustrated by Lucy Corvino

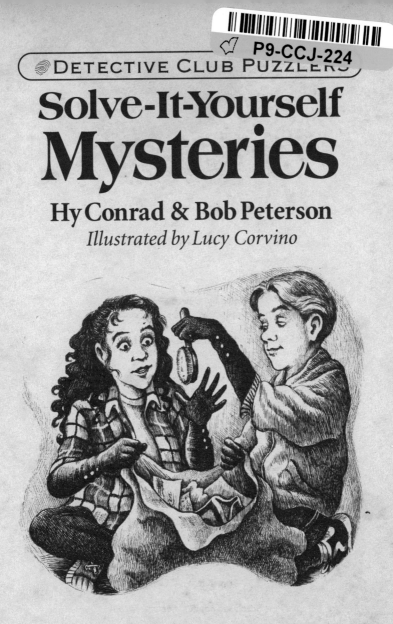

SCHOLASTIC INC.

New York Toronto London Auckland Sydney
Mexico City New Delhi Hong Kong Buenos Aires

Edited by Jeanette Green
Carrie's map on page 68 by Bob Peterson

ISBN 0-439-32820-9

12 11 10 9 8 7 6 5 4 3 2 1   1 2 3 4 5 6/0

Printed in the U.S.A.   40

First Scholastic printing, September 2001

❧ Contents ❧

❦ INTRODUCTION ❦

GREG RYDELL AND CARRIE INGRAM are best friends, and they love to play detectives, real detectives, who use genuine police methods to solve real crimes. That's why they formed the Detective Club, so that they could investigate all the mysteries that pop up around their suburban Washington, D.C., neighborhood.

To solve their first case, Carrie borrows a book from her father, a police officer. *The Crime Solver's Handbook* teaches them techniques for taking fingerprints, analyzing blood spatters, tailing a suspect, and more. These methods are useful when the young detectives dive into a summer that's full of cases: a simple jewelry theft, a con game, and even an actual murder.

Solve-It-Yourself Mysteries follows Greg and Carrie through three adventures and seven solve-it-yourself crime stories. After reading each story, it's up to you to solve the mystery, then to look up the solution.

If you want to play detective yourself, investigating mysteries around your own neighborhood, look through *The Crime Solver's Handbook* at the back of the book. It gives you instructions on how to do everything from tailing suspects to making footprint casts.

Maybe you can be as good a detective as Greg and Carrie. Let's find out.

❧ Fingerprinting Fools ❧

HERE IT WAS, LYING in the box on top of an old book and a red shawl. Carrie couldn't resist. She picked up the gold brooch, then walked over to the bedroom's full-length mirror.

"Trying on Aunt Mimi's jewelry?"

Carrie turned with a start and saw Greg's mom standing behind her. "Dr. Rydell!" She stammered and blushed and returned the brooch to the cardboard box.

"Pretty, isn't it?" Dr. Rydell said with a smile. "My aunt is so forgetful. She spends one week with us and leaves behind enough to fill a packing crate. Oh, Greg, can you do me a favor?"

Greg had followed his mom into the guest room. "The usual box for Aunt Mimi," he guessed. "You want me to take it to the post office?"

"No hurry," Dr. Rydell said, as she used a roll of clear packing tape to seal the box. "I'd do it myself, but I'm late for the hospital. You remember Aunt Mimi's address?"

Greg nodded. How could he forget the address of his favorite aunt, crazy Aunt Mimi, who made her chauffeur drive around in her own private yellow taxi cab?

An hour later, Greg and Carrie were in the upstairs den, playing the private detective game Greg had gotten last Christmas. Carrie was a full year older than Greg. They lived just three doors from each other and had been best friends ever since they could remember.

"I'm tired of playing," Carrie sighed and put the tiny magnifying glass back in the game box.

"Me, too." Greg's face brightened. "I know. Let's go mail the package."

It was a sunny summer afternoon. They raced down the hall to the guest room and Greg won. That made him the first to see it, an open cardboard box and an empty spot on the red shawl where the brooch used to be.

"It's gone!" he gasped.

Carrie was right behind him. "The brooch!" she yelped. She pushed past him and dove into the box, rummaging through to the bottom. "It's gone!" she echoed in a whisper. "Maybe your mom took it out. Or your sister."

"Mom went right to the hospital. As for Becca ..."

Greg led the way downstairs where Rebecca and her friend Alicia were on the living room phone and the kitchen extension—talking to boys, of course. Greg made a point of annoying his older sister, so she wasn't surprised when he interrupted their latest bout of giggling and demanded to know how long they'd been in the house.

"We got here right before your mom went to work," Alicia growled.

"Was anyone else in the house?" Greg asked. Rebecca went back to giggling on the phone. "Becca!"

"Rebecca," she corrected him for the hundredth time. "Um. Yeah. Eddy next door. He dropped over to get back some video you borrowed from him."

"Did he go upstairs?"

"I don't know. Can't you see we're busy?"

Carrie put on her sweetest smile and tried her own strategy. "Did you see that terrific brooch your Aunt Mimi accidentally left here?"

The older girls looked blankly at each other, then at Carrie.

"It was upstairs in a box in the guest room. Maybe you saw it? Or borrowed it?"

Rebecca shook her head. "The only brooch I ever saw Aunt Mimi wear was some old-fashioned gold thing. No wonder she left it behind."

* * *

"What are you doing?" Greg asked. Carrie had gone home for lunch and Greg hadn't realized she had come back. But here she was again in the guest room, sitting on the floor by Aunt Mimi's box. A small make-up brush was in one hand, a container of black powder in the other.

"Dusting for fingerprints," answered Carrie.

"Cool." Greg plopped down by her side, fascinated.

"You can't tell anyone about the brooch, not until we get it back. Your mom saw me playing with it. She'll think I took it."

"No." Greg thought again. "Well, maybe. I can't believe anyone would just steal Aunt Mimi's pin."

"Well, it didn't disappear."

"Who do you think took it? My sister? Alicia? What about Eddy?"

"They're our three primary suspects," Carrie agreed. "But first, we need evidence."

"Like real detectives." Greg inspected the open cardboard box. "I don't see any prints."

"You can't see most prints until you dust. It's all in
there." She pointed to a book propped open on a nearby
chair. *"The Crime Solver's Handbook* from Dad's study."
Carrie's father was a police detective. On rainy days, the
two friends liked to sneak a peek at his old manuals.

Greg looked over Carrie's shoulder. She was dusting a
smudge on the sticky side of the clear tape that once held
the top flaps in place. "You found a print," he said, then
lost his enthusiasm. "There must be a ton of prints on that
box: my mom's, yours."

"Not on the inside of the packing tape," Carrie replied.
"I never touched the tape. Your mom touched the ends and
the non-sticky side. Remember? This print has to belong to
the thief." Carrie finished dusting, then used a pair of scis-
sors to cut out the piece of packing tape with the print on

it. She held it up to the light and gazed at the black circular pattern of lines.

"Neat." Greg smiled, then frowned. "I guess we'll need to get fingerprint samples from our suspects. That's going to be hard."

"You don't have to help if you don't want to," said Carrie testily.

"'Course I want to. But how do we get their prints? I mean, without them knowing?"

Carrie sighed, as if it were the easiest thing in the world. "We get a suspect to touch a smooth, hard surface. Then we lift the print." She examined the piece of packing tape and compared it to her own thumb. "It's a thumb. A left thumbprint. I know that from the handbook. All we have to do is get our suspects to touch something with their left thumb. Then we dust and lift those prints and compare them to this tape."

"Sounds easy," Greg agreed. "If we're lucky, we'll get that gold pin back in the box before anyone knows the difference."

Carrie removed the old tape from the flaps and threw it away. Then she took the roll of tape and sealed the box again, making it look just the way it did before the theft.

"Perfect," Greg said. "I'll tell Mom I forgot and that I'll mail it off tomorrow."

Carrie smiled nervously. "Thanks for helping out."

Greg smiled back. "Hey, why not? It's our first real detective case."

* * *

They soon learned how hard being a detective was. They had to actually see the suspect make the print. That was the only way to make sure whose it was. Greg was surprised at how few times people touched hard, shiny surfaces with their left thumbs. It was the next morning before they had their first success.

Greg had found Alicia by the front door, waiting for his sister to come downstairs. "You and Becca going to the mall?" he asked politely.

"What's it to you, dweeb?"

"Oh, nothing. It's just that . . . You know, I didn't think you'd want to go to the mall. I mean, since you have such a big . . . you know . . . a zit."

"A zit?" Her voice erupted with panic as she turned to the wall mirror. "Where? Where's the zit?"

"The light's not very good here," Greg said. "There on your left cheek. Don't touch it. That just makes it worse."

Alicia held her face an inch from the glass. "Of all the rotten luck. It must just be starting. I don't see . . ."

"There." Greg pointed. "That red, blotchy dot. Gross!"

"Oh, no!" She had her left cheek nearly plastered against the glass, touching the surface with her left hand. Greg made a mental note of the position of her thumb. Alicia looked and looked. "I don't have a zit!"

"'Course not, Leesh," Rebecca said as she bounced down the stairs. "I would have told you."

"Oooh! Your brother!" Alicia made a move as if to slap him. "Zits are something you don't joke about."

Greg watched the two girls walk out the front door. Then he turned back to the mirror and broke into a grin.

It was Carrie who took care of print number two. As soon as Rebecca came home from the mall, the young detective followed Greg's sister upstairs, pretending to be interested in fingernail care. Ten minutes later, Carrie walked into Greg's room holding the rounded end of a shiny, stainless-steel nail file. "Nice big thumbprint," she proudly announced.

Greg congratulated her, then reached for the black powder. "The only one left is Eddy. Any ideas?"

Carrie was staring out the window to the yard next door. The whirr of an old-fashioned push lawn mower drifted up into the bedroom. "As a matter of fact, yes."

Eddy had been working for over an hour, if you could call it work. The moody 16-year-old took his time trimming around the flower beds. When Greg and Carrie wandered in through the gate, he was just getting up from a rest break in the hammock.

"Looks like you need a drink." Greg tried not to make it sound sarcastic. Carrie was behind him, carrying two plastic glasses on a tray, one filled with fizzy brown, the other with fizzy orange. "What do you want, cola or orange?"

"Cola." Eddy's eyes were full of suspicion. "What are you up to?"

"Just trying to be nice," Greg answered. "Sorry about not returning the video."

"No problem." Eddy smirked. Carrie was on his left side, forcing him to use his left hand to pick up the glass. Greg drank from the other glass, paying attention to the spot where Eddy's thumb was wrapped around the plastic.

"So, how's it going?"

"Fine." Eddy finished it off in two swallows. Carrie's tray was nearby when he lowered the glass and placing it back there seemed only natural. As soon as the glass was on the tray, the detectives made an about-face and marched straight back to the Rydell yard.

Eddy stood by the hammock, frowning and scratching his head as they disappeared. "Weird little brats."

* * *

Carrie had just lifted the third thumbprint with a clear piece of tape. As she pressed the tape onto an index card and labeled it, Greg took Eddy's plastic glass and rinsed out the sticky scum of orange soda.

When all the index cards were ready, they sat down at Greg's desk and compared, trying to match one of the three thumbprints they collected to the print from Aunt Mimi's box. "There's no match," Greg finally whispered. "They're all different."

"They can't be," Carrie protested. "Let's check again."

They checked again and came up with the same result. No match. "Someone else must have been in the house," Carrie said and threw the useless cards onto the bed. "Oh, Greg. We'll never solve this. Everyone's going to think it was me."

"That's impossible." Greg glanced around his bedroom.

Fingerprinting Fools

Somewhere they had made a mistake. But where? There on his bed were the index cards. Beside them were Eddy's plastic glass, the roll of tape, Becca's nail file and Aunt Mimi's box. Then he started to laugh.

"We're idiots." Greg started to dance around the room. "Total fools. I know where we made our mistake. I know who took the brooch. I know."

Carrie made a face. "How can you know?"

How did Greg know? The answer is right here in the story. When you think you know, too, turn to the solution on page 71.

For hints on how to lift fingerprints, turn to the "Fingerprints" section of The Crime Solver's Handbook, *at the back of this book.*

❦ AUNT MIMI AND THE SWAMI ❦

1. SECRET MESSAGES

G REG LIKED AUNT MIMI. She was rich and full of fun and always involved in some adventure. Like right now, he thought. How many other kids got to visit a real swami and take part in a seance?

It all began when Aunt Mimi telephoned his parents last week, asking if he could come up to New York. "The *most* perfect psychic lives just across the street," she chirped in her birdlike voice. "Gregory has to meet him. I insist." No one ever said no to Aunt Mimi. So, Greg packed a bag and waited for her chauffeur to pick him up in the big yellow taxi to take him from D.C. to New York.

Greg and his aunt sat at a table in the swami's colorful apartment while the tall, dark-skinned man with the turban and pointy beard polished his crystal ball with a cloth. "Mimi, dear," he said in a lilting Indian accent, "We will try once more to contact the spirit guide, Ama. Ama will guide you to your one true love."

"I was writing about love just this morning in my diary," Mimi exclaimed.

"Diary!" the swami repeated as he glanced out the nearby window. "Diary! Well, let's all hold hands and close our eyes." The swami shot his arms out of the sleeves of his robe, grabbed their hands, and began to hum. "Mmmm. Ama! We lowly mortals are in need of your guidance." He was chanting in a singsong voice. It was kind of spooky and silly at the same time, Greg thought.

Even with his eyes shut, Greg couldn't help seeing the bright flash of light. More and more flashes hit his eyelids until finally he gently sneaked them open and looked out the window. Another flash, like sunlight bouncing off glass. It was coming from the high-rise apartment building across the street. Greg could see someone facing them, a

blonde woman standing inside a fifth floor window. Her right hand was raised and light seemed to be blinking from it. Quick flashes followed by short pauses, then more flashes. Dozens of them.

A delicate voice was coming out of the swami now, a woman's voice. "I am Ama, priestess of love. You seek guidance, dear soul. In your diary, you wrote of two men. Two old boyfriends. You wondered if one of these is your true life mate."

"Yes. That's exactly what I wrote," twittered Aunt Mimi.

"I am sorry. Neither man is your destined love. But there is a third, a man named Henry."

"Henry? Henry Posley?" Aunt Mimi's lipstick curled

into a frown. "My one true love? Hmm, I never quite trusted Henry. Maybe I was wrong."

When Greg sneaked his eyes open again, the flashes had stopped. The woman was still in the window, but now with binoculars, her gaze focused on Swami Morishu. Behind the woman, Greg could see the snarling face of Rex, the favorite pet poodle Aunt Mimi had had stuffed and mounted and made into a table lamp. Wait a minute!

Greg blinked and looked again. It was Rex, all right, just as dead and dusty as ever. But if Rex was in the window, then the woman must be in Aunt Mimi's apartment. He inspected the other windows. Yes, it was Aunt Mimi's place. There was her gadget-filled kitchen and his own

Aunt Mimi and the Swami

guest bedroom. The woman moved the binoculars in his direction and Greg snapped his eyes shut.

The seance lasted another half-hour, but he barely listened to any of it. What was that woman doing in his aunt's apartment? And why was she spying on them?

Greg didn't tell anyone about this. But two days later, after it happened again, he got on the phone to Carrie.

"On both days it was the same. The woman, the flashes of light, the binoculars. I didn't say anything. Our sessions are always at noon, when the maid and the chauffeur are out to lunch. So, no one else was in Aunt Mimi's apartment when the woman was there."

"Could be burglars," Carrie said.

"I thought so, too. I asked if anything's been missing lately and she said no. Look, Carrie, I gotta go. Aunt Mimi's cooking her famous octopus fondue. She needs me to stand by with the fire extinguisher."

The next seance was Sunday afternoon. Swami Morishu led them to the table by the window and once again instructed them to close their eyes.

"You wrote in your diary this morning." The swami was speaking to his aunt in Ama's high, singsong voice. "You wrote about love? No. You wrote about friends? No."

As before, the flashes of light hit Greg's eyes and, as before, he sneaked them open. There was the woman again, at Aunt Mimi's window. She held the binoculars to her eyes with one hand. From the other hand came the flashes.

"You wrote about family?" the swami continued. A single flash. "No. You wrote about money?" And, for the first time today, a double light flashed out. "Ah, yes. You wrote about money."

Suddenly it was clear. "She's signaling him," Greg thought. "She's using those binoculars to read his lips, then she's signaling him with a hand mirror. One flash for no. Two flashes for yes."

Aunt Mimi smiled. "I don't usually think about money, but yes. This morning I did."

So, that was it. They were working together. As soon as he and Aunt Mimi left the apartment, the woman sneaked in and started snooping. She read Aunt Mimi's diary, checked old phone messages, went through their bedrooms. That's how the swami knew. He wasn't psychic at all.

A bunch of new flashes. "Will," the high voice said eagerly. "You were thinking about your will."

"Not exactly," Mimi twittered. "I wasn't thinking about *my* will."

This fake and his partner were out after her money. They had to be. But what could Greg do? Just as the next flash hit, Greg jumped to his feet. "I've got a headache," he pouted. And before the swami could stop him, Greg was at the window, pulling down the blinds.

"You can't do that," the psychic yelped suddenly in his real voice.

"Why?" Greg said accusingly. "Are you looking at something out there?"

"No. But I need the sun for my vibrations."

Aunt Mimi's eyes were open and she was rubbing her temples. "To be honest, swami. That flashing sunlight gives me a headache, too. Let's enjoy the shade for a minute. Ama didn't answer my question. Whose will was I thinking of?"

Greg grinned. "Yeah. Tell us about the will. And don't look out the window."

Beads of sweat began to appear under Swami Morishu's turban. "Uh, I can't contact Ama now." He was on his feet now, nervously pacing the floor. Every few seconds he would turn and stare at Greg, as if trying to figure out what the boy was up to. "Let's take a break."

The swami went into the kitchen and made iced tea. They drank it in the kitchen. Every now and then, the swami would bring up the will. But Greg would always change the subject before Aunt Mimi could say anything.

Time passed slowly. Half an hour later, after they'd all drunk their tea, Aunt Mimi was getting impatient. "Ama must be wondering what has happened to us."

Swami Morishu looked sick. And then the doorbell rang. The tall man almost ran to answer it. "Ah," he said from the doorway. "Food delivery. Uh, that's right. I ordered sandwiches from the corner deli. My treat."

Greg caught a glimpse of the delivery boy just before he walked away. Only it wasn't a he. It was a woman. A blonde. In fact, from what Greg saw, she looked exactly like the woman he'd seen at Aunt Mimi's window.

Swami Morishu was in a better mood now. He placed the big brown bag on the kitchen table and invited them to pick out their own sandwich.

Greg reached into the bag, still confused. Could it really be the same woman? And why was she delivering sandwiches? Absentmindedly, he pulled out a folded sheet of paper. Probably a deli menu or a receipt, he thought, and slipped it in his pocket. Reaching in again, he found a ham sandwich.

"Did anyone see ..." Swami Morishu was at the paper bag now, his head nearly buried inside. "Did anyone see a piece of paper? Greg? Maybe when you took out your sandwich?"

Greg almost admitted it but changed his mind. "You mean like a menu? No, I didn't see anything. Why?"

"Oh, no reason." The swami dove back into the bag, tearing out sandwiches and pickles and closely examining the pile of napkins. "Blast," he muttered under his breath. "Are you sure you didn't see a paper? Even a blank paper?"

"Nope." Greg took a big bite of ham, then secretly glanced down at the tip of paper sticking out of his pocket.

* * *

"He got real upset. And then he sent us home. He didn't even try to contact Ama. Aunt Mimi was sure mad." Right before dinner Greg was again on the phone to Carrie.

"They're con artists," Carrie decided. "Working together. Greg, you have to protect your aunt."

"They must have Aunt Mimi's apartment key. But how do they do the signals?"

"One flash for 'no.' Two flashes for 'yes.' When she needs to give him words, like *will*, she probably spells them

out in Morse code. So, what about this piece of paper from the deli bag? What's on it?"

"Nothing." Greg held up the folded paper, as though he were showing it to her over the phone. "Blank. No writing on either side."

"No!" Carrie didn't believe it. "There must be something. I mean, as soon as you closed the blinds, she must have called the deli, ordered a bunch of sandwiches, then written a message to put inside the bag."

"Well, there's nothing on it," he insisted. "Unless it's invisible."

"Ooh. Good idea. Did you check for invisible writing?"

"What? I was kidding. How can writing be invisible?"

"Lemon juice," Carrie reported. "You take a tiny paint-brush, dip it in lemon juice, and write. When it dries, the writing turns invisible."

"Then how do you read it?"

"Simple." And she explained the technique.

Greg made Carrie stay on the line while he went into the living room. He switched on Rex, took off his lamp-shade, and held the paper up to the bulb the stuffed dog was holding between his paws. Brown letters quickly began to appear.

A minute later, Greg was back on the phone. "It's invisible writing, all right. But the message is nonsense. I mean it's in English letters but they aren't real words."

"Hmm. A secret code. The swami and his friend must have worked out a code, just in case something like this happened. Are there any letter patterns?"

"Patterns?"

"Small groups of letters that repeat. Look at the four-letter words."

Greg checked the message. "Yeah," he said, his voice regaining some hope. "The first word has repeating let-ters. XBXB."

"Good, that could be *Mimi*. It took Carrie a few seconds to grab a pencil and paper. When she was ready and back on the phone, Greg spelled out the message.

XBXB FSGCZ HEGWC OZS WLNPZ'K FBPP. OZ JBZJ PHKC DZHS. KOZ BLOZSBCZJ XGKC GQ OBK HKKZCK HLJ BK ZUZL SBNOZS COHL FZ COGWAOC. HXH.

"I'll work on it," she promised. "Meanwhile, take care of Aunt Mimi. This swami guy is up to no good."

Can you read the swami's message? For help, consult the "Codes" section of The Crime Solver's Handbook. *When you think you've correctly decoded the message, turn to the solution on page 72.*

The handbook also contains great information on "Invisible Ink," "Morse Code," and "Sending Messages with Mirrors."

2. Observing the Swami

Carrie stood in front of the swami's apartment building, talking to her new friend, "So, this swami doesn't have a lot of clients."

"Just two," the doorman replied. "There's that crazy rich woman across the street." He meant Aunt Mimi. "And then a nice-looking blonde." Carrie figured this had to be the swami's lady partner. "He never gets any other guests."

"Is that his real name? Swami Morishu?"

"Don't know." The doorman finally looked past Carrie and noticed Greg weaving through the traffic. "Hey!"

Greg had sneaked halfway across the avenue, then hidden himself behind a huge pot in the middle of the street divider. At a break in the cars, he raced across the rest of Park Avenue and started pawing through the bags of garbage on the doorman's curb.

"Hey, kid! What the heck is he doing?"

Before the doorman could move, Greg found what he was looking for. Among all the gray and black plastic, he grabbed the only green bag, then darted back across the avenue. A mail truck honked its horn and swerved. Carrie breathed a sigh of relief as Greg reached the far sidewalk.

"Crazy kid!" The doorman scratched his head. "Stealing garbage. That's a first."

A few minutes later, Carrie walked into Greg's bedroom. Greg had on a pair of long opera gloves that he'd rescued from his aunt's clothing drive donation and was rummaging through the open bag. "I can't believe I almost got run over for garbage. This stuff stinks."

Carrie put on a second pair of opera gloves and joined him. "Don't forget. We're looking for anything that tells us a little more about the swami. Aha!" Her first find was a cigar wrapper. "Panatela," she read, then placed it in a baggie and labeled it.

They had been on the first day of their stakeout, sitting

by a window and using their own binoculars to watch the swami's apartment. Late that morning, when Carrie saw him tying up a green garbage bag, she got the bright idea to steal it.

"No personal mail," Greg said as he sifted through a stack of envelopes. "Occupant ... Occupant ... Hairbrush." He held up a black hairbrush.

Carrie eagerly grabbed it. "Hmm. The swami's hair is black. His partner's is blonde. Yours is brown. Aunt Mimi's is gray." Carrie used tweezers to pick a hair out of the brush then examined it with a magnifying glass. "Red and wavy. What's a red, wavy hair doing in the swami's apartment?"

Observing the Swami   23

Greg wasn't paying attention. He had found two small triangles of foam rubber. The flat end of each triangle seemed to be dyed with a brown liquid. "What are these?"

"Just bag and label it," Carrie said. "I'll look at it later." She herself was busy bagging and labeling the red hair.

"Hello in there. Yoo-hoo." It was Aunt Mimi. By the time she threw open the door, Greg and Carrie had stuffed the garbage out of sight behind the bed. "What's that smell? Gregory, did you brush your teeth?"

"Yes, Aunt Mimi."

"Good. Are you children ready for some adventure?" Mimi's eyes were aglow. "The swami and I just had a session. My spirit guide says today is critical. Ama gave me very detailed instructions. We walk three blocks north, chant to the sun for two minutes, take the first taxi heading west, then . . . Well, the swami wrote it all down. At the end of our journey, at exactly three o'clock, I will encounter my true mission in life. Isn't that just too exciting?"

A few minutes later they were exiting Mimi's building, turning north. That's when Carrie happened to glance across the street and see the swami. He was dressed in a suit but still wore his turban. "This is our chance," she hissed. "I'm going to tail him."

"What?" Greg whispered back. "What am I going to tell Aunt Mimi?" But Carrie was already on her way, disappearing across the avenue, heading south after the turban.

*   *   *

"It's almost exactly three." Aunt Mimi went from checking her watch to checking Ama's list. They had taken three taxis, zigzagged across Times Square traffic while humming "Born Free" and even walked backwards for a block, just so they'd be facing the sun. She and Greg now stood exhausted, somewhere downtown on the Bowery, in front of a small Off-Off-Broadway theater.

"This is obviously our destination." Mimi looked into the box office window and was startled to see a surly young

man with orange hair staring back. "Hello. Is there a show today?"

"If you can call it a show." The orange-haired boy pointed to a sign proclaiming "*The Marigold Prophecy*. A new drama of spiritual importance." "Matinee starts in 2 minutes," he said.

"Wonderful." Aunt Mimi beamed. "The spirits must want us to see it. Three tickets, dear." And then, for the first time since they left Park Avenue, Mimi glanced around. "Where in the world is Carrie?"

"Oh." In all the excitement, Greg had forgotten to tell his aunt about Carrie. Worse, he'd even forgotten to think up an excuse. "Uh, Carrie? She's around here someplace."

"Carrie!" Aunt Mimi shouted. "When did you last see her? You don't think when we were crisscrossing Times

Square . . ." Aunt Mimi shuddered. "Where's a phone? I'll call the police commissioner."

"No," Greg blurted. "I'm sure she's okay."

"Better yet, I know the President's unlisted number." And then her voice suddenly calmed. "Oh, there you are. Carrie, you gave us such a fright."

Greg jumped and turned. There was Carrie, all right, walking around the corner. Before she could reach them, he was racing to meet her. "Thank goodness. How did you know where to find us?"

"I didn't. I was following the swami. He walked into this place 10 minutes ago. I didn't have money to buy a ticket, and I didn't know what to do. The swami's instructions led you here? Very weird."

Aunt Mimi and the Swami

"Carrie, dear, you shouldn't wander off, not even for a minute." Aunt Mimi was standing by the door, waving three tickets. "Well, come on. The play's about to start."

They walked into the theatre just as the lights were fading. Only about a dozen of the folding chairs were occupied. Carrie scoured the audience, looking for a tall head wrapped in a turban and seemed a little confused when she didn't see one.

"I know he came in here."

She was promptly hushed by Aunt Mimi, who was squinting at the program. "It can't be," Mimi gasped in a voice high enough to be a car alarm. A dozen heads turned in her direction. Two dozen eyes glared. And then the curtain went up.

It was the story of man who was searching the world for some rare flower. Along the way, he learned all sorts of lessons about life. The lead actor was a tall redheaded man who overacted a lot.

The whole thing seemed pretty silly. And then the scene changed to a flower shop. The woman behind the counter turned around and Greg instantly yelped, "That's her!" The flower woman was being played by the swami's blonde partner. "An actress."

Aunt Mimi sat entranced by the cheap sets and the bad acting. As the curtain fell on Act I, she turned to her nephew and gushed, "That was Henry Posley. You know, the old boyfriend Ama said was my one true destined love. It's fate. Fate! The spirits have led me to him."

Greg knew better than to argue, but something was definitely fishy. He didn't realize what it was until the second act when Carrie leaned across and whispered, "That red-haired actor. It's the swami."

"No." Greg tried to imagine that face with darker skin, black hair and a turban. "Well, maybe. Those foam pads I found. He could have used them for make-up."

"And the red wavy hair." Aunt Mimi hushed them again and they were forced to sit through the second act in silence.

"We have to go backstage," Mimi said. The houselights had come up and she began marching toward the stage. They ran to catch up, following her through the curtain and back to a row of dressing rooms. The name Henry was scrawled on a door.

Mimi knocked enthusiastically. "Yoo-hoo? Henry? This is a voice from your past."

"Mimi?" asked a voice. "Could that be Mimi Astorbilt? Uh, wait just a minute."

Carrie listened carefully. Someone was moving frantically inside. She could hear footsteps, things being knocked over. What was he doing? Finally, there was a shuffling sound, like something being crammed into a container.

"Darling!" The door flew open and there stood Henry, out of breath. "I saw you in the audience. What a wonderful surprise!"

Mimi led them into the small room and Henry introduced himself. "Ms. Astorbilt and I used to be such great friends— until she got the idea I was after her money. Don't deny it, Mimi. It's normal for a rich woman to have such thoughts." He kissed her on the cheek and she tittered. "After we parted ways, I wrote a play. You were my inspiration. I put every cent I had into this experimental tour de force."

"You wrote it, too?" Mimi checked her program. "Writer, producer, and star. How brilliant." Then she gasped and gazed up to the ceiling. "This is what my spirit guide wants. Oh, thank you, Ama." She turned dramatically. "Henry, we are taking your show to Broadway."

Henry seemed flabbergasted. "Are you serious? Me, on Broadway? But that takes a lot of money."

"And I have a lot of money. The spirits said I would discover my true mission, and this is it, to bring your wondrous play to the world. The spirits have decreed. Was I truly your inspiration?"

"My only inspiration." And he kissed her other cheek.

She tittered again. "What a day! Is there a financial plan I can see?"

"It's right in the office." The eager actor was leading her out the door. "Kids, make yourselves at home. Your aunt and I have business to discuss."

The door slammed shut, leaving Greg and Carrie alone in the shabby dressing room. "That's him," Carrie said and pointed to a cigar in the ashtray. "Panatela, just like the swami."

Greg made a face. "Is she really going to do his show? It's terrible."

"It's all a con." Carrie began searching the cluttered room, turning over scripts and checking under costumes. "Henry and his girlfriend wanted to do their play. That's when he remembered Aunt Mimi. Henry knew she'd give him money, but he had to regain her trust."

Carrie disappeared into the closet and was rummaging around. "So, he disguised himself as Swami Morishu and spent a few weeks predicting her future."

"Hey. What are you looking for?"

"His disguise. When he came here today, he was the swami. His turban and wig and beard—they have to be somewhere."

"Good idea." Greg jumped up. "I'll start from this side. If we can show Aunt Mimi that Henry and Morishu are the same guy . . ."

Between them, they scoured the entire room, meeting in the center. They had found absolutely nothing. "He must have hidden it," Greg said and then snapped his fingers. "Sure. That's what he was doing when we knocked, hiding his costume. But where?"

Carrie eyed the door uneasily. "We'll use our powers of

observation." She forced herself to stop searching and just look. Greg joined her in the center of the room. "He had to hide it in a hurry."

Inch by inch, they examined the dressing room, looking for anything out of place, any clue to the location of the costume. Any second now, Henry and Mimi might return.

Can you find the hiding place? Examine the illustration. When you think you've found the spot where Henry hid his disguise, turn to the solution on page 74.

Consult the The Crime Solver's Handbook *for information on "Hair and Fiber Analysis" and "How to Tail a Suspect."*

3. Canceling the Contract

"Yoo-hoo." It was the most depressed "yoo-hoo" they'd ever heard.

Aunt Mimi sighed her way into Greg's bedroom. "I am so bummed out." She plopped herself onto the bed. "Swami Morishu has left. His own guru called him back to India. He's going to live in a cave and meditate, and I'm not going to have my swami anymore."

Greg was shocked. "You mean he's gone? Just like that?"

"Just like that. Moved out of his apartment this morning." A distant doorbell rang. "Who could that be?" Aunt Mimi slumped out of the room.

Greg turned to Carrie. "What do we do now? I mean,

how do we prove Henry's the swami when there's no more swami? We can't let him just take her money."

Carrie frowned. "There's nothing illegal about getting someone to finance a Broadway show, even a lousy show."

They could suddenly hear voices from the living room, Aunt Mimi and a man. "We'll have an agreement written up, everything legal. After all, we don't want our affection for each other clouding our business judgment." It was Henry Posley, cooing romantically.

Greg and Carrie raced into the living room and found him stroking Aunt Mimi's hair. "Uh, we should hurry to the lawyer's office," Henry said as he worked to pull his fingers from the mass of hairspray. "No need for the children. They'll just be bored."

"We won't be bored," Greg protested.

"Henry's right. You stay home. Now where did I put my purse?"

"I'll get it." Greg ran out of the room, returning a minute later with Aunt Mimi's oversized handbag.

"Is my lucky pen in there?" She grabbed the bag and turned to Henry. "It was a gift from my very first guru. I can't sign any document without my lucky fountain pen."

"I doubt we'll be signing anything today." Henry swept an arm around her shoulder and guided her out the door.

Two hours later, Aunt Mimi returned home and dropped her purse into an empty fish tank. Greg was hiding behind the curtains. As soon as she disappeared, he fished it out and scurried back to his room. At the bottom of the overloaded purse, just where he'd planted it, was a cassette tape recorder. Greg rewound and pressed play.

The first few minutes consisted of the ride downtown in Arthur's cab. Once they arrived at the lawyer's office, the sound got better. Henry introduced her to Jordan Harsh, a contract attorney, and Henry outlined the agreement they wanted. Aunt Mimi would put up all the money for *The Marigold Prophecy*, $3 million. "We want the best production possible," Henry said.

When Mimi heard the price, she hesitated, "That's an

awful lot. Perhaps my business manager should look at this."

Henry clucked his tongue. "He'll talk you out of it, I'm sure. Businessmen don't understand. I thought, when the spirits guided you to me, we could avoid all that negative nonsense."

"Yes, of course," Mimi apologized. "This isn't a business venture, it's a mission. All right, three million."

The lawyer worked out the details. Greg didn't know much about business, but it sounded like a pretty bad deal to him. "I can have it written up by tomorrow," Jordan Harsh announced. "Two P.M. And Ms. Astorbilt, please bring a checkbook. On signing, you'll need to pay Mr. Posley half a million dollars."

Carrie wandered in and Greg played the entire tape again. Then they sat on his bed trying to figure out what to do.

"Tomorrow," Greg moaned. "What can we possibly do by tomorrow?"

"We have to do something," Carrie said. "Is there some grown-up who can help us? Maybe one of her friends?"

Greg made a face. "Aunt Mimi has weird friends. Like this gourmet chef. Cal Encino. He lies all the time. He's her best friend, knows everything about her, but you never know when he's telling the truth."

* * *

Chef Cal Encino looked down at the spoonful of rice, then up at Greg. "You want me to chew on uncooked rice?"

"Please. It's a school project," Greg explained. "We're trying to see if people with sensitive tastes can tell the difference in uncooked rices. My Aunt Mimi says you have the best taste buds in New York."

The chef smiled. "In all North America. When I was 15, I won an international tasting competition. Youngest winner ever. And I had a cold."

They were in the kitchen of the chef's cafe. Carrie had laid out three spoons of uncooked rice, all looking the same. In fact, they all were the same, from the same rice box. But that wasn't the real point of the test. "Just put each spoonful in your mouth. Chew it a while. Then tell us which is the best."

Chef Encino smiled and followed directions. As soon as he started chewing the first portion of rice, Greg was ready with a question. "So, do you know Henry Posley? He used to be Aunt Mimi's boyfriend."

"Mmm," the chef mumbled between chews. "Real nice fellow. An actor. Got married a few months ago."

"What?" Carrie blurted. "He's married?"

"Someone important told me. I think it was the mayor. I'm done with this sample." Carrie handed him a bowl and watched carefully as he spit the rice into it. "Dry," he said and reached for a glass of water.

"No," Carrie said. "No water."

"Ah. More of a challenge, huh? Very well."

Aunt Mimi and the Swami

As soon as the second spoonful was in the chef's mouth, Greg continued. "Who did he marry? An actress?"

"Yeah. Some actress he knew before Mimi. A blonde. Mm, better texture. Nutty flavor." And he spat out mouthful number two.

Carrie had read about this in a book. It was an ancient Chinese lie detector. You make your suspect chew on uncooked rice. If he's lying, then his nervousness will cause his digestion to slow down. His body will stop producing saliva and he won't be able to spit out the rice. But Chef Cal Encino was spitting out rice just fine.

"Is he telling the truth?" Greg whispered as the chef picked up the third spoon. "I can't tell."

"It's not really a foolproof method," Carrie admitted. "But I'll bet Henry is married—and to his blonde partner."

"Number three is the best," Chef Encino said as he chewed. "Reminds me of the rice I used when I cooked a special banquet for the very last emperor of China." And he easily spat out the third sample.

* * *

All during lunch they worked on Aunt Mimi, trying everything from a toothache to tea leaves to get her to cancel the meeting. "Your horoscope says it's a bad day for signing things," Greg told her.

"Nonsense. I checked my horoscope. It's a great day. Now where's my lucky pen? Has anyone seen my pen?" Aunt Mimi's voice echoed as her head vanished into her huge purse.

"Here it is." Carrie walked into the room, wiping off the gold fountain pen with a towel. "You left it in the bathroom."

"Huh. Why was I using my lucky pen in the bathroom?" Mimi tossed it in her purse. "Is everyone ready? Today is the day Mimi Astorbilt becomes a Broadway producer."

Arthur and his yellow taxi-limousine were waiting, and within minutes Mimi and her young friends arrived at the lawyer's office. Henry was already there. "Oh. You brought the kids." And his manner became more defensive.

It was over quickly. The lawyer reviewed the contract. Every now and then Henry would eye Greg and Carrie suspiciously, but they simply sat on the couch, not saying a word. They continued to sit silently as Aunt Mimi brought out her lucky pen. She signed the last page with a flourish, then wrote out a check for half a million dollars.

Once they were out of the office and back in Mimi's private taxi, Greg spoke up. "Remember that errand I needed your help with?"

"Oh, yes," Mimi replied. "We'll do it right away. Arthur? Do you know where the Marriage License Bureau is?"

"Yes, ma'am. Centre Street. Don't tell me you and Mr. Posley are . . .?"

"Oh, no," Mimi giggled. "Not yet, anyway. You see, Carrie's cousin ran away from home. They think the young man moved to New York and got married. Our junior detectives are trying to track him down through his marriage records. Isn't that right, Carrie?"

"Uh-huh." It was amazing the things they could get Aunt Mimi to believe. "His name is Henny Iosley."

"Odd name," Mimi mused. "And somehow a little familiar."

The records were stored in the city clerk's office, a large room that was crowded with romantic couples applying for licenses. Aunt Mimi explained that they needed to look up a marriage certificate. The clerk nodded and had Carrie fill out a yellow form. "That'll be 15 dollars," he told them.

Aunt Mimi turned over the money. "Just check the records for this year," she said, trying to be helpful. "Henny Iosley."

The clerk checked the name Carrie had written. He looked up, a bit puzzled. Then he shrugged and disappeared into a back room.

Ten minutes later he returned with a photostat copy of a marriage certificate. "You were right," Mimi crowed. "One step closer to finding your cousin. Is there an address listed?" She grabbed the paper and started reading. "What a coincidence. Your cousin lives on the same street as

Henry. Lives in the same building. Hmm." Her eyes roamed up the form and checked the name at the top. "Clerk." She was irritated. "Clerk! You looked up the wrong person. We don't want Henry Posley's marriage certificate. We want ... Oh. Oh, dear! Henry can't be married."

Greg watched her struggle with the proof that was staring her straight in the face. He should have felt happy about their plan working so well. Instead, he felt sorry.

"Henry's married," she finally said. Her voice wasn't weak or teary. It was strong and angry. "Why, that rat. Married! He was using me. Sweet-talking me into backing his idiotic play. Sorry, Carrie, we'll look up your cousin some other day. Where's a phone? I have to cancel that check."

Aunt Mimi almost flew, the sleeves of her dress flapping like wings. She found a pay phone in the lobby and was soon talking to the vice president of her bank. She gave him the check number, the name, and the amount. "Stop payment," she ordered and hung up. "Good." Then her victorious grin faded.

"What's wrong?" Greg asked.

"I signed something, didn't I?" Mimi sat herself down on the marble floor, opened her purse and pulled out her copy of the contract. "Oh, my," she murmured as she read. "According to this, I have to finance his play. There's no clause letting me change my mind. Oh, Gregory. Why did I ever sign?"

For the first time, Aunt Mimi looked defeated. Her wrinkled face, usually held up by a smile, was sagging into her neck. Greg couldn't resist a smile. "You tell her," he said to Carrie. "It was your idea."

A glimmer of hope flashed in Mimi's eyes. "What idea?"

"You don't have to pay anything," Carrie said proudly. "You never really signed the contract."

"Of course I did. There's my signature in dark blue ink."

"No, it isn't," Carrie laughed.

Aunt Mimi stared at her. "What have you children been

up to? This is one of your little detective thingies, isn't it?" She was smiling again. "Tell me, tell me. I really don't have to pay off that smarmy con artist? How in the world did you manage it?"

How did Greg and Carrie foil Henry's con game? The method they used is described somewhere in The Crime Solver's Handbook. *When you think you've figured it out, turn to the solution on page 75.*

Consult The Crime Solver's Handbook *for "Lie Detecting Methods."*

❧ SUMMER CAMP ALIENS ❧

1. The Disappearance

THE FULL MOON DUCKED behind a cloud. Good. Greg and Carrie took deep breaths then popped up from behind the rock and ran.

Carrie kept one hand up, protecting her face from the oncoming branches. Out of the corner of her eye, she saw something move. In that bush. She turned her head, all the time still running. "Greg?" But Greg was ten feet ahead and pulling away. "Someone's there." And she stopped.

Greg looked back. The moon was just emerging. "Run. You're a target." But it was too late. He saw her gasp as the force of the shot snapped back her head. Suddenly Carrie's face was a blob of red. Red liquid covered her eyes and dripped down her cheeks.

Greg pressed himself flat against a tree. He didn't dare look, didn't dare move, not until he heard the killer's gleeful peel of laughter and the footsteps running away. Then he scrambled back to Carrie's side. "Are you all right? I mean for being dead?"

Carrie was taking off her goggles, wiping her face, and doing her best to keep the paint from getting on her jacket. "I hate this game."

This was Greg's first year at summer camp and Carrie's second. One of the big events was a nighttime game of capture the flag. Camp Potomac divided itself into red and blue teams. Each camper was given goggles and an armband, while each team was supplied with ten paint guns. The paint guns usually went to boys, older boys with a few summers' worth of experience.

"Looks like someone got killed," a voice called out. Greg spun around, ready to dive for a rock. But it was only Ping Lao, Greg's tentmate, sporting a blue armband, just like theirs, and a blue paint gun. Ping was a year older than Carrie, a nice guy who loved pranks and practical jokes even more than Greg. "What're you doing way out here?"

Greg pointed to the fence. "We were hoping to scoot outside camp property and in again at the archery range. It's right by the red flag."

"Highly illegal." Ping was planning to be a lawyer like his father, head legal counsel at the Chinese embassy. "I like it." He bent down and refastened the adhesive bandage that covered a cut on his leg. "That's the McGruder farm," he added, gazing beyond the fence. "You guys aren't scared to go there? You know, all the ghost stories they tell around the campfire."

"Please!" Carrie laughed. "That's just their way of keeping campers off his land."

Summer Camp Aliens

"Oh, yeah? What about that guy a few months ago? Some old hermit just disappeared. Without a trace."

"Wow!" Greg was getting the chills. "You think the ghosts got him?"

"There are no ghosts," Carrie sneered. "Anyway, the rules say I have to go back. Have fun." And she walked away.

A mischievous twinkle appeared in Ping's eye. "Well, Greg. If you're not scared of a few ghosts, neither am I. You ready?"

"What? You wanna go with me?" Greg was suddenly partners with an old pro, and a shooter, too. "All right!" He let Ping take the lead, following him over the wooden fence and into a new set of woods.

Five minutes later, they came out on a hill overlooking

a lake they'd never seen before. They were somewhere on McGruder's farm. Lost. They strained to see some trace of the camp, but nothing looked familiar. A dog snarled and barked in the distance and Greg remembered the campfire stories about Old Man McGruder's wolfhound. His skin began to crawl.

It was Ping who first saw the humanlike creatures. All four were floating, maybe even walking, across the mist-covered lake. Large white heads with bug eyes and huge round mouths. Their bodies too were white, almost glowing. Ping gulped. "Wow! Aliens."

"Aliens?" Greg was stunned—and a little relieved they weren't ghosts. On the shore, a red light strobed from a shadowy machine. "Look. More. Coming out of the ground."

Not far from the machine, two white heads had popped up, followed by bodies that slowly climbed out onto the scrubby soil. Not human. They could see that much, despite the spinning red light and the mist. "Wow," Greg said and this time his voice carried.

One of the aliens looked their way. There was no place to hide. The creature pointed right at them and a white light flashed from his finger. Ping and Greg both felt frozen, caught in the beam. Then, somehow, they managed to turn—and run.

* * *

Carrie was dubious. "There's got to be a logical explanation."

"Yeah? What?" Greg challenged. "You didn't see them. We did."

They hadn't told the counselors. Their fear of breaking the rules was, for now, stronger than their fear of aliens. All three of them sat huddled in Greg and Ping's tent, the boys telling and retelling what they saw and trying to figure out what to do.

"All right, boys. Lights out," a grown-up voice bellowed out of the darkness. It was Todd Grisham, Toady Todd, the water sports counselor. He came closer. "Who is that? Lao? Rydell? You guys have a girl in there?"

Summer Camp Aliens

After taps, girls and boys had to stay separate. Those were the rules. Todd did his expected bout of yelling, then marched Carrie across to the girls' side of the camp. Greg and Ping watched them disappear, then switched off their flashlights. "We'll talk in the morning," Greg yawned, "when our heads are clear. What a night, huh?"

* * *

Anna Fox, the crafts counselor, sat in the doorway of her tent. She hailed Greg as he passed. The heavyset woman had just finished making a pair of moccasins and her mouth was still full of rawhide laces that needed to be cut. "Where's your tentmate?" she chewed.

"Don't know. He wasn't around when I got up."

"Hmm. Ping said he would help me with the lanterns for

tomorrow's campfire. It's not like him to stand me up." She pulled her head back and the laces went taut. "Give me your pocketknife." Greg didn't have one. So, with her free hand, Ms. Fox pulled a lighter from her pocket, flicked the flint, and singed through the laces. "Just like a Native American," she said proudly. "They didn't have pocketknives either."

At the mess hall, Toady Todd was taking roll. That's when they discovered Ping was missing. Ten senior campers fanned out across the Potomac property and each returned with the same story. No one had seen him all morning.

The sheriff's office took the news seriously. "There was a local man who vanished three months ago," the sheriff explained. "Never found. I know this missing kid is a bit of a prankster. But we're treating this as a real disappearance, maybe even a kidnapping."

Greg had his own ideas. What if the aliens had come and disintegrated Ping? Or taken him back to their planet? Greg ran off to confer with Carrie. He found her at the pond, dangling her legs in the water.

"Don't be an idiot," Carrie said as nicely as possible. "There are no aliens. I'll bet anything he just sneaked onto McGruder's farm and got lost. We should go back up to the lake and look for him."

"Yeah. Good plan," Greg said, even though going back to the lake was the last thing he wanted to do. He was about to say something else when there was a rustle of branches coming from a row of lilac bushes. A faint scent of cigarette smoke mixed with the lilacs and, for a moment, they felt uneasy, as if they were being spied on.

They didn't have a chance to put their plan into action until after lunch.

Carrie brought her copy of *The Crime Solver's Handbook* and met Greg by his tent. She was surprised to find him 10 yards from the edge of the meadow, on his hands and knees, pawing through the dirt. "What are you doing?"

Greg looked up, excited. "Remember the cut on Ping's leg?" He pointed to a small drop of dried reddish black on the dusty ground. "What do you think?"

"Blood," she said under her breath and began to look around for more. "A blood trail." Greg joined her and in less than a minute they'd found another circular drop, this one on the leaf of a sumac sprig. "He went this way."

Carefully, they lined up the two drops and went in a straight line, following one of the many paths through the woods. Every 20 yards or so, they would find another drop. Some were easily visible on rocks. Others were on leaves or on the ground. Occasionally, there would be no drop for 40 to 60 yards, then they would find several bunched together.

"We're going the wrong way." Carrie came to a halt and scratched her head. "We're heading away from the McGruder farm. Why would Ping come this way? It doesn't make sense." She pulled the handbook from her pocket and began to flip through.

"I found another one," Greg called out and waited for her to catch up.

They examined the new blood drop, spread over a few pebbles. Like the others, it was symmetrical and relatively round. "They're fakes," Carrie announced.

"What do you mean, fakes? You mean Ping planted these blood drops?"

"Not Ping. Someone else. Someone who wants us to go in this direction. Blood doesn't make this shape, not unless it's falling straight down and the person's standing still. Here. Read this chapter."

Greg read it through twice and nodded. "You're right."

"Someone is leading us off on a wild goose chase."

Greg frowned. "I don't get it. I mean, what's the point? Why would someone want to send us on a false trail?"

"Yeah," Carrie agreed. "What's the point?"

They lowered themselves onto a tree stump and thought. If someone was making a false blood trail, that meant Ping didn't just get lost. Someone had done something to him and was now trying to lead people away from the real location.

"You think someone kidnapped him?" Greg asked. "You think maybe the aliens?"

"There are no aliens," Carrie growled. "Someone heard us. Someone—a human—was in the bushes and heard us planning to go to McGruder's. The person didn't want us going there, so he set up this phony trail."

"Let's go tell the sheriff," Greg said and led the way back along the trail. When they emerged onto the quadrangle of platform tents that made up the boys' field, a dozen officers were spread out on the nearby grass, bent over and inspecting the ground. "Uh-oh," Greg said. "They found it, too."

A moment later, the camp director saw Greg and Carrie. "This area is closed to campers right now," Lucas Miller told them. "The sheriff's men found something."

"It's fake," Carrie interrupted. "You found blood drops, right? Well, they're fake. It's a wild goose chase to make you go the wrong way."

Mr. Miller was one of the good guys, friendly and usually willing to give you the benefit of the doubt. Now he didn't look so friendly. "Did you make these blood drops? Is that what you're saying?"

"No," said Carrie. "But we examined them. They're too round and even. Someone wants to lead you in the wrong direction."

"Carrie." Lucas Miller was rubbing the light brown stain on the inside of his middle finger. "You're a smart girl. But why don't we leave the police work to the police?" And without another word, he shooed them off the field.

"I hate it when people don't listen," Carrie muttered. "Come on." She was already leading Greg across the camp, to the pond and the lilacs. Pushing aside the leafy branches, she began to inspect the ground. "Aha! A fresh footprint, in the middle of a lilac bush! I told you someone was spying on us." A cigarette butt also caught her eye. "Whoever spied on us is a smoker. Probably a counselor, since they're pretty careful about keeping cigarettes away from campers."

Greg picked up the butt. "Good work. Now what counselors do we know who smoke?"

Which counselors smoke? Test your powers of observation by trying to solve this one without reviewing the story. And remember, you don't have to actually see someone smoke to know he's a smoker. When you think you know, check the solution on page 76.

Consult The Crime Solver's Handbook *for more information on "Blood Evidence."*

2. The Rescue

Ping was slowly coming to. He tried to open his eyes but couldn't. He tried to speak but couldn't. What had the aliens done to him? His head ached and his mind was so groggy. Last night . . . what happened last night?

He had waited until Greg was asleep. How could anyone sleep with aliens just over the hill? Ping certainly couldn't. It didn't take him long to find the lake. It looked so peaceful. No mist. No strobe lights. No aliens.

"Who are you?" It was a deep, Darth Vader voice, processed through some kind of breathing apparatus. Ping spun around, caught a glimpse of the white figure—bug eyes, hockey-puck mouth—and he was off, dashing past the alien, stumbling down the hill. And then he fell. That was the last thing he remembered: the fall. And now he couldn't open his eyes or mouth or . . .

Ping calmed himself. No, he wasn't mute and blind. He was gagged, bound and blindfolded. He was indoors, probably in a barn, judging from the smell. Then he heard the voices.

"The men finished last night," someone whispered. "It's all buried, safe and sound." The other voice was too soft to make out. "'Course it's safe. You think I'd let them plant all that toxic waste on my property if it wasn't?" Was that Old Man McGruder? "You saw all the cement. These guys are pros. Besides, they paid me enough. I'll retire and sell the farm. You think your campers would like a new field full of toxic waste?"

"Your campers?" Ping wondered. "Who is he talking to? Someone from the camp?" He suddenly smelled a cigarette.

"Don't smoke in my barn. How much do you think the kid saw?" Another pause. "Well, we can't take any chances. It won't be the first time we got rid of a nosy neighbor. Hey, don't get squeamish. You had your chance to be a hero. Instead you took their money." McGruder laughed and Ping's skin crawled. "The police are following that fake blood trail. By the time they check out the farm, that Chinese kid'll be buried with the waste."

Ping sat frozen. Then the voices were gone. Nothing but the contented shuffling of cows. Ping moved his head around until it nudged up against something hard and metallic. It was a rake. He maneuvered it under the edge of his blindfold and pulled. After several tries, Ping moved the blindfold enough to catch a peek.

The first thing he saw was a skinned alien. No. His heart settled. Just a white, plastic suit hanging from a peg. It was the kind of protective suit that covered your whole body, with bug-eyed plastic goggles and a round filter over the mouth. They weren't aliens, just environmental polluters.

Ping thought it through: Take away the mist and the spooky night, and all you had were a bunch of men in boats and earth-moving machines, burying toxic waste and checking things out with a high-powered flashlight. He felt stupid and a little disappointed.

*　*　*

Greg and Carrie never found the lake. Instead, they found a house and barn. Coming to the edge of a field, hidden from view by cornstalks, they watched as someone drove away in a Camp Potomac pickup. A craggy-looking man was sitting on the porch, a rifle resting on his knees. Sleeping beside him was a wolfhound. McGruder's dog. Greg was more afraid of him than of the man himself.

Rain clouds were coming fast and the last rays of sun were just lighting up the barn. Then they saw it: a flash. It was a dull flash, barely noticeable. Then again. On the third flash, they pinpointed the source, a barn window. Greg undid his knapsack and pulled out binoculars. "There's someone inside, at the window."

"Yeah, a cow."

"No, a person."
A fourth flash, then
the sun was swallowed
up in clouds. "It came from his mouth." Greg adjusted the
binoculars' focus and felt a raindrop. "It looks like there's
some shiny tape on his mouth." Greg's voice cracked. "It's
Ping." The wolfhound on the nearby porch pricked up his
ears and began to growl. "Let's get back."

They retreated into the corn, then sat down and
planned Ping's rescue. "We need a diversion, something
to keep the man and the dog busy." Greg peered through
the stalks and saw a herd of cows wandering up to a pond.
"Hmm." He reached into his knapsack and pulled out a
paint gun.

His diversion took another five minutes to organize. A
heavy rain began falling as Greg crawled back to the edge
of the field. Carrie was right behind him. "This isn't going
to hurt them," he promised. "You ready?"

The gun popped softly. A blue blob exploded on the rear
end of a Guernsey, and the cow reacted with a terrified

moo. The cows around her also reacted. A second pop, and a second blue blob splattered over two more cows. More terrified moans and moos. By the fourth paint ball, the herd was in full panic, colliding with each other as they stumbled away from the cornfield.

The old man was suddenly on his feet, looking almost as panicked as the cows. "What's the matter? Calm down." Meanwhile, the dog was off the porch and barking furiously.

The frightened herd settled on a direction, toward the house, and they were gaining speed. "Hey!" The man waved his arms, then scrambled for his rifle and fired a shot in the air. The dog howled. A chorus of moos, the loudest yet. The stampede veered to the right, away from the house, thundering through a vegetable garden. The snarling dog followed, saliva flying from his mouth.

The man cursed, running after them into the rain. That's when Carrie took off across the grass and into the barn. It took her only seconds to find the window and climb in to rescue Ping. She tore the tape from his mouth and started working on the ropes. "They were going to kill me," the older boy sputtered. "What's going on out there?"

Carrie didn't explain but led him to the barn door and listened, her eyes focused down. A nearly unsmoked cigarette lay stubbed out on the floor. A used match lay a few inches away. "One of the counselors was here," Ping whispered. "I couldn't see which one."

Carrie nodded. "That was way cool, the way you used the tape as a signal."

"What signal? I was trying to look out the window."

"Well, it was still cool." Carrie poked her head through the barn door. "Let's go." And they raced away.

By the time the campers had finally sneaked their way back to the other side of the fence, the downpour had stopped. Along the route, Ping filled them in about McGruder and the toxic waste. Greg was amazed by Ping's story and couldn't wait to tell the police. Rescuing the son of a Chinese diplomat and exposing a band of toxic dumpers—they were heroes.

Summer Camp Aliens

But things don't always work out. Greg knew something was wrong when he saw the man, Mr. McGruder, getting out of a pickup truck. His hands were covered in blue paint as he started talking to the sheriff and Lucas Miller. The men all saw the campers and didn't look happy.

"There they are," McGruder shouted. "I found one of them, that Chinese boy, hiding in my barn. He'd been there all night. I grabbed him for trespassing. He kept talking about some practical joke. I was just going to call the camp when this other crazy boy, he starts shooting at my cows with a paint gun." He pointed to Greg, who was still carrying the weapon.

Mr. Miller frowned. " Did you shoot paint at his cows?"

"Yes," Greg stammered. "But it was self-defense."

"They kidnapped Ping," added Carrie. "They were going to kill him."

"Kill him?" Mr. Miller looked shocked. "Why in the world . . .?"

"Because of the toxic waste," Greg blurted. "McGruder and one of the counselors are in it together. We thought they were aliens. That's why we didn't tell anyone. But they weren't aliens, just men wearing special suits to bury the poison." Greg had a feeling of how stupid this sounded, but he kept going. "When Ping sneaked back to the farm, they kidnapped him. I had to shoot the cows as a diversion."

"Lucas?" The sheriff cleared his throat then gazed at Ping. "Is this the same boy who set off the fireworks in the girls' latrine last year?"

"Yep," said Mr. Miller sadly. "Your parents aren't going to be very happy."

Greg, Carrie, and Ping all protested their innocence. "Go look on his farm," Carrie demanded. "Down by the lake. It's buried there, tons of toxic waste. All the proof you'll need."

"Shut up and go into the mess hall," the sheriff ordered. "We'll deal with you in a minute."

It was a half-hour later when Toady Todd Grisham walked in to get them. "I hear you guys are in big trouble," he said gleefully. "Serves you right for missing my canoe races."

"Canoe races?" Greg had forgotten about the races, Todd's favorite event of the week.

"Yeah. And don't say you skipped it because of the rain. It didn't start raining until we were nearly through. They want you losers out by the flagpole. Now."

The sheriff and a deputy were waiting and quickly escorted the campers to the roped-off area around Greg and Ping's tent. As the sheriff untied the rope, Greg looked down and noticed the footprint. "Someone's been in our tent," he whispered.

Carrie saw it, too, an adult-size print outlined in the mud just outside the left flap. She hurried ahead, then stopped, preventing anyone from stepping on it. "Wait out here," the sheriff ordered, then walked around her into the tent.

The sheriff started his search from one side, the deputy from the other. When the deputy got to Greg's toilet kit, he inspected it carefully, then motioned to his boss.

"Okay, boys. Game's over." The sheriff reached into the kit, pulling out a small bottle of red liquid and an eye-dropper. "Is this is how you made the blood drops?"

Greg was stunned. "That's not mine, honest. I've been framed."

"Framed? You been watching too much TV."

"No." Greg pointed to the footprint. "You see that? That's proof. Someone was here after the rain stopped. They crossed the police ropes and planted that in my kit."

The sheriff wasn't listening. "We'll have this analyzed to see if it matches what's on the trail. Offhand, I'd say you three are facing expulsion, maybe even criminal charges." He and his deputy walked off, leaving Greg, Carrie, and Ping to worry about the future.

"This isn't fair," Ping complained. "They bury tons of poison, kidnap me, try to kill me, and *we* get arrested. Greg, what are you doing?"

The younger boy was bending over the footprint. "There must be some way to use this print as evidence. Where's the handbook?" Carrie pulled the thin book out of her pocket. Greg took it, sprawled out on his cot and found the right page. "We'll make a cast of the footprint and compare it to everyone's shoes."

"We probably should make a cast," Carrie agreed. "But we already know who the crooked counselor is."

Greg was amazed. "And how do we know that?"

"Process of elimination," she replied. "We know a few more things about our suspects now. I think we can safely eliminate two of them."

Can you eliminate two of them? Review the story and see if you can narrow it down to one suspect. When you think you know, check the solution on page 77.

Consult The Crime Solver's Handbook *for information on "Footprint Evidence."*

3. The Evidence

Greg brushed the last clumps of dirt from the plaster cast. "It's a Supersonic Flyer," he confirmed, pointing out the double "S" in the tread. "A new pair, too."

Without exchanging a word, all three campers thought of the new pair of Supersonic Flyers that had arrived for Lucas Miller in Monday's mail.

"It's not him," Ping shouted. "It can't be. I don't care what your footprints say. You don't know Mr. Miller. I've come here three summers and . . ."

Something splattered against the canvas, shaking the whole tent and making them jump. "Hey,

Ping Pong," someone yelled. They knew that bullying voice—Butch Cleaver, a fourth-year camper and captain of the red team. "Played one too many jokes, huh? Your folks are coming for you." No one answered and no one looked outside to see what he'd thrown.

They thought it through and came up with a plan. The best way to prove their story was to expose the toxic waste. "We'll go back to the lake and do some digging," Ping suggested. "All we have to do is hit the top of the cement. People are bound to wonder why McGruder buried a patch of cement by his lake."

It was late afternoon when they packed up the knapsack and slipped out under the tent's rear canvas. "How about a paint gun?" Greg whispered.

"Paint gun?" Carrie scolded. "That's how we got into this mess." But both boys insisted, and they started their mission by making a detour to steal a red paint gun from the supply tent.

Ping led them directly to the lake and they quickly found the large area of freshly turned dirt. Even though the toxic waste was buried under a mound of concrete, Carrie made them put on breathing masks and plastic gloves before they started. They took turns with the shovel, pitching out mounds of earth until they had a waist-deep hole.

It was Ping's turn to dig and he stopped when he heard the noise. "What's that?" They all listened. It was louder now. A dog barking. Angry barks that grew louder and closer. "Oh, no! McGruder's dog."

Suddenly there it was, barreling from around the edge of the woods. It saw them as soon as they saw it and dug in its heels, stopping just 20 feet away. The shaggy wolfhound faced them, saliva dripping from its teeth and its back hairs bristling.

For a minute nothing happened but the snarling and barking. Carrie saw Greg out of the corner of her eye. He was looking at the paint gun. "Greg, don't. He knows guns. He'll attack before you can even aim." Then she turned to Ping. "What are you doing?"

The older boy had taken off his mask and was inching toward the knapsack. "I'm going for a cupcake."

"How can you eat at a time like this?"

Ping reached into the sack as he continued to stare down the dog. "Nice boy," he said gently. "Chinese dogs are always hungry. You hungry?" Slowly, he pulled out a cupcake, unwrapped it, and held it out. "Doggie treat." He lobbed it with an underhand swing and it fell a few inches in front of the muddy, matted forepaws.

The dog sniffed at it, then snapped his head up, as if he were expecting some kind of trick. "Poor thing. Probably been mistreated. It's okay, boy."

The wolfhound sniffed again, then in one quick motion snapped up the cupcake. "Good boy," Ping said. "Want another?" The dog cocked its head and seemed to smile.

A second cupcake followed the first, followed by three strips of beef jerky. All the while, the dog never moved except for the few inches it took to reach the treats. "No more," Ping finally said. "Sorry. Please don't eat me."

The wolfhound cocked its head again and whined. Then, as quickly as it appeared, the dog whirled and bounded off.

Summer Camp Aliens

As it vanished behind an abandoned shack, the kids came to life.

Carrie sat down on a rock, her knees still wobbly. "I guess we keep digging. You'd think we would've found something by now." And it was just then she did find something. It was lodged deep in a berry bush, a faded red baseball cap, cracked and torn by the weather.

Greg bent over the bush. "Probably one of the toxic dumpers," he said. But Ping reminded him that they'd been wearing a different kind of headgear. "Well, then, probably McGruder. Looks like it's been here for months."

Carrie was still wearing gloves as she picked up the cap and placed it in a large plastic bag. "It could be evidence. You guys keep digging. I'm going to make a crime scene sketch."

"What?" Greg complained. "What good will that do?"

"For later. To remind us how things are situated—where we found the cap, et cetera. The police do it all the time."

Carrie retrieved her pencil and sketchpad from the knapsack, sat back down on her rock, and drew. It took some time, since she wanted to make everything as accurate as possible. She was just returning her pad to the knapsack when the dog bounded down towards them again. "Oh, no. He's coming for more food."

Ping squinted. "No. He's already got something."

Once more the dog came to a halt, this time under an oak tree. The thing in its shaggy mouth was long and white, with knobs on both ends. "Like a baton," Carrie thought, and then her stomach turned. "It's a bone."

"He wants to play." Ping moved a foot closer, but the dog curled its lip and snarled.

"I wouldn't get too close." Greg grabbed Ping by the belt and pulled him back. The wolfhound lowered its lip and dropped the bone. Then it barked once, whirled around, and galloped away.

The bone had fallen onto a patch of grass and leaves. "Looks like a leg," Carrie deduced. "Too long and straight for an animal bone."

The boys knew what she was implying. They both made faces. "That's gross," Greg said. "I suppose you'll want to bag this, too?"

"Uh-huh." Carrie pulled out the largest bag, using it to pick up the bone. Some debris was sticking to it. "Dry gravel, dry soil, dog hair, oak leaf, raspberry thistle." She tried to get all of it into the bag, but the gravel and soil were so dry that much of it wouldn't stick. These bits she also saved, slipping them into a sandwich bag.

The sun was now low in the sky. They were tired and hungry. "I don't think we can dig down far enough to find the cement," Ping said, defeated.

Carrie and Greg agreed and started to pack up. "What if it *is* a human bone?" Carrie asked. "You know, that local guy who disappeared a few months ago?" She was trying to cheer them up, but it wasn't working.

They removed their masks and gloves, then headed back

to camp the same way they came. Soon they could see the fence and, with a rush of relief, they moved toward it.

"Stop right there!" It was a voice from their nightmares. McGruder's voice. "You kids never learn, do you?" He was right in front of them, stepping out from behind a tree. A rifle was slung over his forearm. "What're you doing on my property?"

"Nothing." Ping's voice quivered and his grip on the knapsack tightened.

McGruder saw this and smiled. "Nothing, huh? Put down the gun." It took Greg a second to realize he still had the paint gun. He lowered it to the ground. "What you got in the backpack?"

Before they could even reply, he shot out an arm and grabbed the knapsack. Then he sat on a stump and opened it, all the time using his free arm to keep the rifle aimed. "Now what have we here?" Feeling around inside, he pulled out a plastic bag and held it up to the fading light. "An old cap. Looks like . . ."

His smile vanished. He eyed the campers warily, then reached in again. Another plastic bag, this one almost as long as the knapsack. "A bone," he said. For the longest time he sat quietly, his gaze going back and forth between the plastic bags and his prisoners. When he finally spoke, his voice was hoarse. "Where did you get these?"

"Down by the lake. Where you left them," Carrie answered, half-guessing.

McGruder looked as if he'd just been punched. "How'd you know about Sammy?"

Sammy. Carrie figured that had to be the local man who disappeared. She turned to Greg. "I told you it was a human bone. Sammy must've seen the toxic dumpers, too."

McGruder jerked to his feet and cocked the rifle. "Pretty darn smart. All right, girlie, put the stuff in the bag. Careful and slow." Carrie did as she was told.

"McGruder! What the heck are you doing?" The three youngsters turned their heads and saw Lucas Miller climbing over the fence. The camp director seemed to take

instant control of the situation. "Put down that rifle."

Ping grinned and nudged Carrie. "I told you," he said. "Mr. Miller, am I glad to see you."

"Shut up," Lucas Miller barked.

McGruder was still aiming the rifle. "I guess our burial spot wasn't so good, Miller. They stumbled over Sammy's remains."

"Blast," Lucas said. "I never bargained for this kind of mess."

Even though they had deduced that Mr. Miller had to be the crooked counselor, the kids were still shocked. It was during this shocked silence that Greg saw his opportunity and took it. He lunged forward, grabbing the knapsack with one hand and preparing the other to catapult himself over the fence.

In a second, he was inside the camp and racing down a wooded path. Every hundred feet or so, the paths would split and one after another he took new paths, almost without thinking. Any minute now, he would run into a counselor and be safe. They wouldn't kill Carrie or Ping, not until they caught him.

A few more quick turns and he hit a clearing. Then came the ravine and the rope bridge. Greg glanced down at the rocky creek below, then up at the opposite bank. Farmer McGruder was standing there, out of breath but smiling, with his rifle at his side. "Throw me the backpack, boy."

Greg looked behind him for escape. But the wolfhound was suddenly there, snarling, its forepaws on the edge of the ravine.

"Looks like you're caught between a man and his dog," McGruder laughed. "Rufus, shut up!" Rufus snarled more than ever. "Okay, boy, throw me the sack and I won't have to shoot."

"You won't shoot," Greg yelled.

"Oh, I'm not aiming at you. I'm aiming at Rufus. Everyone knows how mean that dog is. You see, Rufus just attacked you. I'm trying to save your life. Unfortunately, I'm gonna miss him and hit you. Now time is running out. Throw me the sack."

"No." Greg could hear people shouting somewhere in the distance.

"All right, boy. I hate to do this. Gunshots drive that dog crazy." In a skillful sweep, McGruder raised the gun and aimed. Rufus saw the gun being pointed in his direction and, sure enough, went crazy.

Greg barely saw what was happening, it was all so fast. One second the dog was there, frothing at the mouth; the next second he was scrambling down the ravine and up the other side.

"No, you fool mutt." McGruder threw down his rifle and raised his arms to his neck. But the dog was already on him, everywhere on him, a swirl of snarling and biting.

McGruder's screams were muffled by his arms, making it easier for Greg to hear the shots. "Pop! Pop!" Rufus's backside was suddenly covered in red. "Pop! Pop!" Two more red bursts appeared, one on McGruder's chest, the other on the dog's head.

Rufus ran off in a whimpering, whiny confusion while McGruder slumped to the ground, still screaming for his life. "You shot me. I'm dying."

Greg spun around and recognized the shooter standing on the far bank. "Carrie!"

"I still hate this game," Carrie said as she lowered the paint gun. "But I *am* pretty good at it."

* * *

Greg's and Carrie's parents drove in that evening, expect-

ing to find their children expelled. Instead, they found the camp director in handcuffs and the sheriff in a serious conference with the members of the Detective Club.

The sheriff was acting friendlier than Carrie had ever seen him. "I sent your bags off to Washington. A forensic geologist will study the stuff on the bone. That'll help us figure out where to dig for the body." He cleared his throat. "Mind me asking what that is?"

Carrie had unfolded her crime scene sketch. "It's a map I drew. The area where we found the cap." She looked up. "I examined the bone before I bagged it. And I think I know where the body is."

"How can you possibly?" The sheriff controlled himself. "Well, far be it from me to second-guess the Detective Club. Would you kindly share your insights with me?"

The Evidence   67

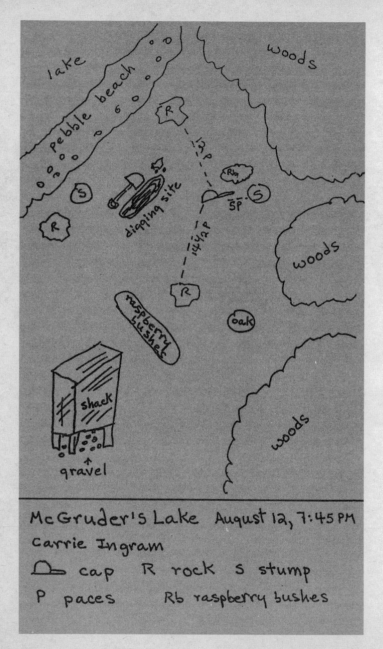

McGruder's Lake   August 12, 7:45 PM

Carrie Ingram

⌂ cap   R rock   S stump

P paces   Rb raspberry bushes

Examine Carrie's sketch and compare it to the evidence she saw on the bone. Can you discover where Sammy's body is buried? When you think you know, check the solution on page 78.

Consult The Crime Solver's Handbook *for more information on "Crime-Scene Sketches."*

❧ SOLUTIONS ❧

FINGERPRINTING FOOLS SOLUTION

Greg picked up Eddy's index card. "This is *my* left thumbprint, not Eddy's."

"What?" Carrie's face brightened. "Are you sure?"

"Positive. We must have mixed up the glasses. Eddy drank the cola. I had the orange soda. Remember?" Greg turned to look at the tray and the empty cola glass on top of it. "Eddy's print is on that glass. And I'll bet you anything . . ."

Five minutes later, they had dusted and protected and examined the new print. It perfectly matched the tape from Aunt Mimi's box.

With this evidence in hand, they finally went to Greg's mom and told her everything.

Dr. Rydell examined the prints and listened to their story. "I'll go have a talk with Eddy's mother. I wouldn't have suspected you anyway, Carrie." She put the index cards in an envelope. "How did you do it? You kids have some sort of detective club? Is that it?"

"Detective club," Greg said with a gasp. "Cool idea."

"Very cool," Carrie agreed. "We can even call it the Detective Club. There must be lots of mysteries around town to solve. We'll get some friends to join us—the smartest ones."

"I get to be club president," Greg demanded.

"What?" Carrie asked. "Why you?"

"I solved the first mystery; so, I get to be president."

"Now you kids be careful," Dr. Rydell warned. "I don't want you getting into trouble."

"'Course not," Greg and Carrie said in unison. Trouble? They were both grinning at just the thought of trouble.

"Aunt Mimi and the Swami"

1. Secret Messages Solution

The next morning, Carrie called back. "I cracked it," she said breezily. "I figured the first word had to be *Mimi*. That gave me two letters. Then I found a word that was probably *will*. The most used letter in the message I guessed had to be *E*. After that it was a lot of trial and error, like playing 'Wheel of Fortune.'"

"So? What does it say?"

Carrie cleared her throat. "'MIMI WROTE ABOUT HER UNCLE'S WILL. HE DIED LAST YEAR. SHE INHERITED MOST OF HIS ASSETS AND IS EVEN RICHER THAN WE THOUGHT. AMA.'"

Greg wrote it all down. "Wow! Wait till I show this to Aunt Mimi."

His aunt was in the living room, spraying a haze of underarm deodorant all over the mirrors. "It hides wrinkles," she said. "Makes me look younger. What do you have there?"

Greg let her read it for herself, then tried telling her the whole story. How the swami had a partner who broke into her apartment and sent messages. How they were con artists out after her money. But the more Greg explained, the more Mimi was unconvinced.

"You're wrong. This message is from Ama. When we got our headaches, Ama had to find some new way to contact me. Invisible spirit writing, that's what it is."

Greg grabbed the paper and read the last sentence aloud. "'She inherited most of his assets and is even richer than we thought.'"

Aunt Mimi smiled. "Yes, indeed. I inherited Uncle Frank's love of life, his curiosity, even his brown eyes. And I'm a richer person for it."

Greg gave up. "She doesn't believe me," he reported to Carrie a few minutes later. "What are we gonna do?"

Carrie thought for a second. "We have to find out what

Swami Morishu is up to. Maybe I should come up to visit."

"Great. Aunt Mimi wants you to come and there are plenty of bedrooms. I'll ask her to send Arthur and the taxi."

"This will be our second detective case," Carrie reminded him. "And this time I get to be president."

"AUNT MIMI AND THE SWAMI"

2. OBSERVING THE SWAMI SOLUTION

It was Greg who noticed the tile. At first he didn't realize exactly what was wrong with it. Then he got excited. "Hey. Henry must have been in a hurry to hide his disguise."

Carrie nodded. "You heard him rushing around in here."

"Right. So, maybe he made a mistake. You know, put the cubbyhole lid on backwards."

Now Carrie got excited. "What are you looking at?"

Greg walked over to the wall. "There's one piece of tile upside down." A Boy Scout knife came out of Greg's pocket. He stuck the blade beneath the tile and pried. It flipped off easily, the entire, thin square. Underneath was a natural hole, filling up the 6 inches between the panel and the real wall. "Wow! I was right."

"Wow!" Carrie was just as surprised. "He must have found it by accident, probably when he started using this dressing room. Great hiding place." She reached inside, pulling out a white turban, a black curly wig, and a beard. "Wait till we show this to Mimi." Carrie put on the wig and turban and began to dance around. "I am the great Swami Morishu."

Greg didn't laugh. "I don't know. Henry might have an explanation."

"What?" Carrie stopped dancing. "How can he explain the swami's stuff hidden in his dressing room?"

"He can say he didn't know how it got there. Or it's a costume from some other play. Aunt Mimi can believe almost anything. And once Henry knows that we know about his con game, it'll be a lot harder to stop him."

"I guess you're right," Carrie sighed. She was already returning the disguise to its cubbyhole and closing it up. "At least we know his secret now."

Greg shrugged. "Yeah. We'll just have to find some other way of putting the swami out of business."

3. CANCELING THE CONTRACT SOLUTION

Carrie tried to start from the beginning. "We knew Henry was a con artist."

Mimi wagged her finger. "Ha! You also said the swami was a con artist."

Carrie groaned. "He was. Swami Morishu and Henry Posley are the same man."

"Oh." This was news to Mimi and it took a moment for it to sink in.

Greg took over, explaining everything from the mirror signals to the disguise in Henry's dressing room. "Someone told us he was married, but we had no proof, not until we checked city records."

"Why didn't you warn me?" Aunt Mimi asked. "Why did you let me go and sign that stinking contract?"

"We tried to stop you," Carrie said. "Luckily, we had a back-up plan. We filled your fountain pen with disappearing ink."

"Disappearing?" Mimi looked down at the contract. "Nothing's disappeared. My signature is still there."

"It takes time. You'll have to stall. Tell Henry the bank made a mistake and you'll write him a new check. In three days, you can tell him the truth. He'll take out the contract and your name won't be on it anymore."

Aunt Mimi thought this over and approved. "You saved me $3 million." She smothered them both with big, wet kisses. "You're totally wonderful," she gushed. "And so was my first guru."

Greg was miffed. "What's a stupid guru got to do with this?"

"Everything. He told me this was a lucky pen. And he was absolutely right."

1. THE DISAPPEARANCE SOLUTION

It wasn't easy picking out the smoking counselors since the camp discouraged them from lighting up in front of the campers. In fact, Carrie could think of only one smoker she'd actually seen. "Toady Todd. Remember? I saw the glow of his cigarette when he came to kick me out of your tent."

Greg came up with a second name. "Anna Fox."

Carrie was skeptical. "I'm in the crafts building a lot. I've never seen her smoke."

"She keeps a cigarette lighter in her pocket. It's a good bet that someone who carries a lighter around is a smoker."

Carrie had to agree. "Okay. Anyone else? Oh." She'd just thought of something. "Smokers sometimes have nicotine stains. Did you see that brown stain on the inside of Mr. Miller's middle finger? That's how most people hold cigarettes, between the index and middle fingers. He must be a heavy smoker."

The detectives wracked their brains, reviewing a mental list of counselors and one by one eliminating them. "Bill the cook hates cigarettes," Greg recalled. "Ruins your taste buds, he says. And I saw Terry in the office chewing nicotine gum. That means she quit cigarettes and is trying to stay off them. Anyone else?"

"That's it. Three. Three smokers who could've overheard us talking." Carrie shook her head. "It's hard to believe that one of them kidnapped Ping."

"You know what's even harder to believe?" Greg swallowed hard. "That one of them is an alien." Carrie punched him on the arm. "Ow. I'm serious."

"There are no aliens. Whatever you saw has some perfectly logical explanation."

2. THE RESCUE SOLUTION

"So, who's the crooked counselor?" Ping asked.

"We should get started on your footprint cast," Carrie said and hurried across the field toward the crafts building. "I'll tell you as we go."

"We can eliminate Toady Todd," Greg said reluctantly. "If he was at the canoe races when the rain started, then he couldn't have been with McGruder at the barn."

"Very good," Carrie said. "Hello? Ms. Fox?" She rapped on the door and a second later, the hefty crafts counselor appeared, an unlit cigarette dangling from her lips. "You kids are in deep trouble."

"We didn't do it," said Carrie.

Ms. Fox grunted, then took out her pocket lighter and lit up. "I thought you'd be under tent arrest."

"Not yet. But just in case, can we have some crafts stuff to work with? We'll need plaster of Paris . . ." Carrie rattled off a list of things they needed.

Anna Fox felt sorry enough not to question any of their requests. She motioned them inside, pointed out the supplies, and watched as they carried them away.

Ping was thoughtful for a few seconds, then nodded. "Cigarette lighter."

"Right," Carrie said and explained for Greg. "The counselor in the barn used a match to light his cigarette. That eliminates Ms. Fox."

"Cool," Ping said. "So that leaves . . . Oh." He stopped in his tracks. "The camp director, Mr. Miller. It can't be. He's such a great guy."

"And he runs the whole camp." Greg sighed. "We *are* in deep trouble."

3. THE EVIDENCE SOLUTION

Carrie spread her sketch out on a table and pointed to the oak tree. "This is where Rufus dropped the bone. Your forensic people will find lots of microscopic stuff, but the big stuff was dry gravel, dry soil, dog hair, an oak leaf, and raspberry thistles."

"And that tells you where the body's buried?"

She ignored the sheriff's skeptical tone. "The dog hair doesn't help us. And the leaf probably came from when he dropped it. The raspberry thistle is interesting. Maybe Rufus pulled the bone through some raspberry bushes."

"You want us to dig under all the raspberry bushes?"

"No. We have a much better clue." She paused, trying to make it sound dramatic. "The dry soil and dry gravel."

The sheriff snorted. "Of course there's soil. And the pebbles could come from anywhere."

"Not pebbles," Carrie said. "Gravel. *Dry* gravel. Remember the downpour? The gravel and soil should have been wet, not dry."

"You're right." He gazed at the sketch. "Ah," he said and pointed at the shack. "You drew this shack on pylons. Is the floor of the shack really off the ground?"

Carrie nodded. "About 8 inches. Pylons are often set in a gravel foundation. I can't see any other site that's protected from the rain. Dogs love to dig under things. And look: raspberry bushes, standing between the shack and where he dropped it."

"Uh, excuse me, Carrie. I've got a phone call to make."

Within a half-hour, the sheriff had a search warrant. A half-hour after that, his men were tearing up the shack's floorboards. They didn't have to do much digging underneath. The wolfhound had already unearthed most of the remains of Sammy Glover.

THE
CRIME SOLVER'S
HANDBOOK

*A Basic Reference Manual
for Detectives in the Field*

Codes

Criminals and spies may use secret codes in order to disguise their messages.

There are two main types of code. One is a *transposition code*. That's where all the right letters are there in the message, just mixed up. The easiest transposition code is simply writing the message backwards. If a secret message contains a lot of unusual letters, a lot of Q's, for example, then it's probably not a transposition code.

The second basic type is a *substitution code*, in which every letter in the message is a substitute for the real letter. In order to crack a substitution code, you have to go through the message carefully, substituting letters by trial and error until the words start making sense.

Here are some tips for solving substitution codes.

- The most often used letter in the English language is E, followed by T, A, O, and N. Find the most used letter in your message and try substituting an E for it.

- The most common letter beginning a word is T.

- The most common letter at the end of a word is E.

- A one-letter word is almost always A or I.

- The most common two-letter words are OF, TO, and IN.

- The most common three-letter words are THE and AND.

- The most common four-letter word is THAT.

- Q is always followed by U.

- See any double letters? The most common double letters are LL, followed by EE, SS, OO, and TT.

Invisible Ink

Any citrus juice—lemon, orange, lime, or grapefruit—can be used to make invisible ink. Onion juice also works. To write a

message in invisible ink, use a small brush rather than a stick or fountain pen. A stick or pen can leave pressure marks. After writing your message with the juice, be sure to let it dry properly.

To recover an invisible message, heat the paper slowly over a hot light bulb. The message will turn brown. Be careful not to singe the paper with the bulb. *Never use fire.*

Sending Messages with Mirrors

To send a mirror message, you must keep two things in mind, your *light source* and your *target*, the person your want to receive the message. In most cases you will want to use the sun as your source. If the sun isn't shining, or if it's night, a nearby lamp will also work.

Take a small mirror. Face it directly toward the light source. From this position, slowly tilt the mirror until it's facing halfway between the light source and your target. If the sun is

The Crime Solver's Handbook

bright, a flash of light will land on your target. Practice tilting the mirror back and forth until you can make a long or short flash of light whenever you want. If you're using a lamp or the sun is not bright, don't worry. Your target will be able to see the flash even if you can't. It just takes more practice on your part to line up the mirror.

Try it with a partner. Use Morse code. Or make up your own simple code, such as *four flashes* means "Come quickly."

Write out what you want to send ahead of time and ask your partner to write down what he or she receives. Work on accuracy. With a little practice, you will be able to send almost any message using nothing more than a small mirror.

International Morse Code

This is the most commonly used code in the world. After flashing each letter, pause slightly. When receiving a message in Morse code, write down the dots and dashes. You'll have plenty of time later to translate them into letters.

A ·–	B –···	C –·–·	D –··	E ·	F ··–·
G ––·	H ····	I ··	J ·–––	K –·–	L ·–··
M ––	N –·	O –––	P ·––·	Q ––·–	R ·–·
S ···	T –	U ··–	V ···–	W ·––	X –··–
Y –·––	Z ––··				
1 ·––––	2 ··–––	3 ···––	4 ····–	5 ·····	
6 –····	7 ––···	8 –––··	9 ––––·	0 –––––	

Disappearing Ink

Disappearing ink can be easily made from three ingredients: water, iodine, and starch. Iodine can be bought from a drugstore, while all-purpose cooking starch is easily found in most grocery stores. Combine equal parts water, iodine, and starch. Mix well; otherwise the starch will not properly dissolve and will leave a grainy residue. The finished mixture will resemble a blue-black ink.

Disappearing ink can be applied with a narrow-tip brush or with a refillable fountain pen. If using a fountain pen, try not to write with too much pressure. Excess pressure will result in pressure lines on the paper. In about three days, the ink will completely disappear.

Dusting for Fingerprints

Take a clean fingerprint brush. A make-up brush will also do. Roll the brush handle between your hands to separate the bristles. Now inspect the surface to be dusted at different angles of light. This may make a latent print visible to the eye.

Dip the brush lightly into fingerprint powder, barely touching the powder. Apply a dusting of powder to the surface using light, even strokes. Any smudge that appears may prove to be a print. To clean the print, gently brush it, being sure to go with the flow of the ridges. Gently blowing on the print can also remove excess powder.

Now take a roll of fingerprint tape. Transparent tape can also be used. Pull out enough tape to cover the area (usually 5 to 6 inches), holding the roll firmly in one hand and the tape end in the other. Secure the tape to the area above the print; then slide your thumb along the tape, forcing it down gently over the print. Hold the roll tightly in the other hand. Carefully, smooth down the tape over the print, forcing out all the air bubbles. The print is now protected.

To lift the print, slowly pull up the roll end of the tape until the entire tape is removed. Attach the taped print to a fingerprint card, again being sure to smooth out all air bubbles. Cut off the excess tape and promptly label the fingerprint card with the exact location, date, and time of the procedure.

Fingerprints can be easily lifted from any hard, smooth surface. Glass, metal, and hard plastic are good places to look for prints.

Identifying Prints

No two people have the same fingerprints. And each finger on a person's hand is different from the others. You and everyone else in the world have ten unique prints. This makes it very important to distinguish which finger you are trying to match. The prints found most often are from the index and middle fingers of the right hand. Thumbprints are the easiest prints to identify. Look at your own hand. At the top of your right thumb, you will notice that the ridges flow up and away from the fingers. The same is true for your left thumb.

Fingerprint patterns can be divided into arches (plain arches and tented arches), loops (radial loops and ulnar loops), and whorls (plain whorls, double loop whorls, central pocket loop whorls, and accidental whorls). This makes eight basic patterns. Sixty percent of all prints are loops, while 35 percent are whorls.

First look at the print you need to match. Identify which of the eight patterns it falls into (see diagram). Once you establish this, you can proceed. If a suspect's print does not match this basic pattern, you can eliminate him.

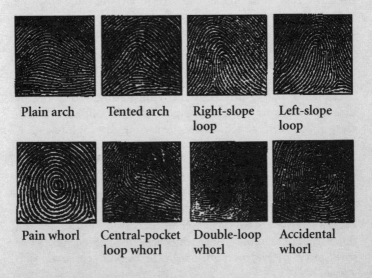

| Plain arch | Tented arch | Right-slope loop | Left-slope loop |
| Pain whorl | Central-pocket loop whorl | Double-loop whorl | Accidental whorl |

If a suspect's print does match your print's basic pattern, the job of elimination becomes harder. You must now look for identification points.

Compare the unique identification points of the suspect's prints with the same areas of the print you need to match. Even one point of difference between prints can eliminate that suspect.

Elimination Fingerprints

Elimination prints are taken directly from a subject's hands and are kept on file for future reference. To take elimination prints, you need an ink pad and a card with room for ten fingerprints and notations.

Have the subject wash his hands. Then take him by the wrist, instructing him to relax his hand and arm muscles. Roll the left thumb on the ink pad, making sure to roll it toward his body. Be sure to hold the four fingers back so they are not accidentally inked. Immediately repeat this rolling process on the proper space on the print card. Repeat this with the four fingers of the left hand. In the case of fingers, roll them away from the subject's body, not toward it. Do the same with the right hand, thumb first, then fingers.

Many police departments also record palm prints. To take a palm print, ink the subject's entire palm and all his fingers. Then press the entire hand straight down on a card. Use a different card for each hand.

If an ink pad is not available, elimination prints can be taken the same way as latent prints. Have the subject roll each clean finger onto a card. Allow the card to dry for a few minutes. Then dust the prints with fingerprint powder and protect with fingerprint tape.

Hair and Fiber Analysis

Everywhere we go, we leave behind hairs from our bodies and fibers from our clothing. At a crime scene, the police gather these small pieces of evidence, often with the help of special vacuum cleaners, in the hope of determining who has been on the scene.

Even with the most advanced equipment, the police can rarely say positively that a hair or fiber came from a specific person. However, even without advanced equipment, you can still make a few deductions through careful examination.

First, is your sample a hair or fiber? Examine it with a magnifying glass. A hair gets narrower from the shaft to the tip. Hairs also have different textures from fibers. Examine several human hairs from different sources. Place each hair against a white background. You'll quickly be able to determine color, texture, curliness, length, maybe even dandruff or other characteristics. Using this evidence, you won't be able to make a positive identification, but you will be able to narrow down your field of suspects.

Treat fibers the same way. Again, you will not be able to state positively that the fiber you're examining came from a certain sweater or blanket. But you will be able to narrow down the field and maybe make a few reasonable deductions about who has been on the scene.

Blood Evidence

NEVER EXPERIMENT WITH BLOOD: NOT WITH YOUR OWN BLOOD—NOT WITH ANYONE ELSE'S.

Investigators can learn a great deal from blood, starting with the species of animal.

If the blood sample is human, then investigators can test DNA (deoxyribonucleic acid). DNA is the basic chromosome pattern that makes you look the way you do. Every person in the world has a different DNA pattern. By testing blood for DNA, police can identify the person that a drop of blood came from, sometimes with 99.99 percent accuracy.

Due to scientific advances, more and more can be discovered from blood all the time. Police are now able to determine these things.

- the position of persons or objects at the crime scene at the time of the attack

- the distance the blood fell and its speed

- whether the blow was from a sharp or blunt instrument

- the number of blows

- the movements of people at the scene after the attack

- the time between the attack and the examination

- whether a bloody wound occurred prior to a fall or as the result of a fall

Even if a perpetrator has wiped blood away, investigators can still see it by the use of Luminol, a chemical spray. After an area has been sprayed with Luminol, a fluorescent lamp will show traces of blood that would otherwise be invisible to the naked eye.

It's also important to note that bloodstains are not always red. Especially when dry, blood can appear black, green, blue, even grayish-white.

By examining the shape of a bloodstain (the blood spatter pattern) a great deal can be learned about a crime. For instance, a small, thick stain indicates that the blood fell a short distance. A larger, thinner stain means it fell from a greater height.

If blood falls straight down from a wound, the spatter pattern will be more or less symmetrical. If the drop looks like a bowling pin or an exclamation point, it means that the body was moving at the time it was bleeding. The smaller end of the drop points in the direction the bleeder was moving.

Fake Blood

If you wish to experiment with fake blood spatters, make up a batch of fake blood. You can do this by combining water, red food coloring, a drop of blue food coloring, and a dash of corn syrup to thicken it. By using an eyedropper, you can reproduce various blood spatter patterns and examine them.

CAUTION: Food coloring can stain many surfaces. Do not use this mixture on clothing.

Lie-Detecting Methods

There is no such thing as a foolproof lie detector. The polygraph machines used by police measure a suspect's pulse rate, breathing, and blood pressure. When these increase suddenly, the police assume that the person is more nervous and, therefore, lying.

But you don't need a polygraph machine to detect a case of nerves. These cues can also indicate nervousness and possible lying.

- dry mouth and sweaty palms

- refusing to make eye contact with the questioner

- distracted eye movements

- nervous twitches

- a suddenly slower speech pattern

- stammering or pausing significantly between statements

- habitually answering a question with a question

- trying to distract the questioner or change subjects

A favorite police technique is to rephrase the same question over and over in the hope that the suspect will trip himself up in a contradiction.

Crime-Scene Sketches

While photographs of a scene are an essential part of a criminal investigation, they cannot replace a good crime-scene sketch. Both photographs and sketches are important. A photograph records everything, even details overlooked by the detective. A well done sketch, on the other hand, will show only the most important elements and can often help a detective better think through a situation after he leaves the scene. Also, a sketch can better reveal measurements and the relationships between objects.

You do not need artistic skill to draw a usable crime scene sketch. These tips should help.

- Your first sketch, done at the scene, can be rough. Don't worry about straight lines and neatness. Just get the measurements and details right. Later, using tools like a ruler, protractor, and compass, you can draw the finished sketch.

- Include the major items of physical evidence and where you found them. Measure distances as accurately as possible.

- Be consistent. If you are using a tape measure, use a tape measure for *all* your measurements. If you are pacing off distances, then pace off *all* distances.

- Include all critical features of the room or outdoor scene.

- Make the sketch easy to understand. Do not include too much detail.

- Label the sketch with your name, the date, the time, and the location. If you are using symbols or abbreviations in the sketch, include a legend that explains them.

When drawing a crucial object, such as a corpse, use the triangulation method to establish the exact location. This is done by measuring the distance to it from at least two widely separated locations.

How to Tail a Suspect

In order to find out more about a person's habits and acquaintances, it is often necessary to tail your suspect. The primary goals of a tail are (a) not losing track of your suspect and (b) not allowing him to discover the tail. Here are some hints for tailing a suspect.

■ **Stay a safe distance back.** Remain as far back as you can while still keeping your suspect in sight. Half to one block is usually sufficient. In most cases, it's better to lose a tail than to let your suspect know he's being followed.

■ **Be inconspicuous.** Try to blend in. Avoid quick movements. Don't draw attention to yourself by dressing out of place or wearing a wild disguise. If the suspect knows you, try wearing clothes of yours he hasn't seen. Something as simple as a different cap and dark glasses can change your appearance from a distance.

■ **Use reflective surfaces.** If you have to get close to your suspect, avoid looking directly at him. Instead, use reflective surfaces, such as a store or car window, to keep an eye on his movements.

■ **Be aware of peripheral vision.** In many cases, a suspect will be able to see you without looking directly at you. This is called *peripheral vision*. Even if you're off to one side, your suspect may be able to see you out of the corner of his eye.

■ **Practice.** Try practicing with a friend. Tail him without letting him know you're there. See how long you can do it without being discovered. See how closely you can tail him before he sees you. This will teach you how far you have to stay behind a real suspect.

Footprint Evidence

Footprint evidence can be an important part of an investigation. Even in the best of circumstances, however, it doesn't give the detective a great amount of information.

Athletic shoes have the easiest soles to match. If you are working with a clear print of an athletic shoe, you can usually determine the shoe's brand, model, and size. If you see no wear or variation in the pattern, then the shoe that made the impression is probably fairly new. If there is a distinctive wear pattern in the impression, however, you will have a better chance of matching your print to a particular suspect's shoe.

Photograph a footprint before you take a plaster cast of it. Carefully remove twigs, leaves, or other debris. A ruler should be placed directly above or below the footprint to indicate scale. If any mistakes happen during the casting process, you will have the photograph as evidence.

Before taking a cast, make sure the print is not overly wet. If you cannot wait for the natural drying process to occur, use a heat source, such as a portable hair dryer. Make sure not to bring the heat too close to the print. Do not let the dryer blow directly on the print since this may damage it. And don't let the print become too dry. This will cause flaking and will damage the print. It should be just dry enough to hold the plaster of Paris.

Set up a metal frame around the entire print, pressing it gently into the soil. This will keep the print from expanding or changing shape during the casting process.

Mix plaster of Paris according to the directions on the box. Be aware, plaster hardens fairly quickly. Use a rubber mixing bowl if you can, since plaster will not stick to rubber. If no rubber bowl is available, use any clean bowl that can be thrown out.

Start with the amount of water you think would comfortably fill the footprint impression. Add plaster and mix, continuing to add plaster until the mixture has the thickness of pancake batter.

Pour the plaster continuously, starting from one end of the

footprint and working toward the other. This will help avoid air bubbles. Do not pour the mixture directly from the bowl into the impression. This can damage it. Always use a spoon or spatula to break the plaster's fall. The overall thickness of the finished cast should be 1 to 1½ inches (about 2.5 to 4 cm).

After pouring in the mixture, reinforce the cast. The best material to use is wire screening, cut into 2-by-4-inch (5-by-10-cm) strips. Imbed these in the wet plaster. This will help prevent the cast from breaking when you remove it. If you do not have wire screening, green twigs can be used instead.

In 30 minutes the cast should be hard. Remove the metal frame, then lift the cast, being careful not to bend it. After the cast dries for another 30 minutes, use a soft-bristle brush to remove any soil clinging to the bottom.

Now you can compare your finished cast with the soles of your suspect's shoes.

Index

ABOUT THE AUTHORS
AND ILLUSTRATOR

Author **Hy Conrad** began his writing career as a playwright in New York and was among the first writers of interactive fiction for computer, with The MysteryDisc, Clue VCR, and Abel Adventures. Mr. Conrad is a regular contributor to on-line computer services and has created many popular mystery games for Milton Bradley, Parker Brothers, and other game companies. Other Sterling books by Hy Conrad include *Almost Perfect Crimes, Almost Perfect Murders,* and *Whodunit—You Decide.*

Author **Bob Peterson** grew up in Warren, Pennsylvania, and now lives in New York City, since he believes he would not now be allowed to live anywhere else. This is his first children's book. He works as a freelance producer, writer, and artist as well as a personal trainer. He thanks his mom, dad, family, and friends for their support, and Ms. Straneva for teaching him to read.

Artist **Lucy Corvino** illustrates a wide variety of books for children and adults, including many Sterling mysteries. She especially likes to draw people. Ms. Corvino attended Rhode Island School of Design and has a master's in art education from Columbia University Teachers College. She lives in New Jersey with her husband, three cats, and a dog.